One Hundred and One
BLACK CATS

One Hundred and One
BLACK CATS

by STEPHEN MOOSER

Illustrated by Quentin Blake

SCHOLASTIC BOOK SERVICES
NEW YORK • TORONTO • LONDON • AUCKLAND • SYDNEY • TOKYO

To Etta

ISBN: 0-590-02309-8

Text copyright © 1975 by Stephen Mooser. Illustrations copyright © 1975 by Scholastic Magazines, Inc. All rights reserved. Published by Scholastic Book Services, a division of Scholastic Magazines, Inc.

14 13 12 11 10 9 8 7 6 5 4 3   0 1 2 3 4 5/8

Printed in the U.S.A.

Contents

Uncle Bones

"Blast this gout! My toe is killing me!" My uncle, Captain Bones, limped heavily across the warehouse and flopped down on a pile of canvas.

"This is a fine mess," he grumbled. "Captain Trapp is waiting for me at the Fogcutter Inn and here I am, hardly able to move!"

Captain Bones very carefully worked his sock off his left foot. He held up a bottle of medicine and thrust out his bare foot to me. The big toe looked as swollen as a bear's nose in a bee-hive.

"Trapp sails on the evening tide," he said, wincing as I painted his toe with the stinking medicine. "Trapp's got a package I must have. A package, my boy, that could make us *rich*."

"Rich?" I asked doubtfully. Uncle was full of get-rich schemes. But this time he sounded pretty certain.

"Aye, rich enough to buy the finest whaling ship in New Bedford harbor."

My eyes lit up. "With a place for me on board?"

"Do ye think I'd maroon you here in this drafty warehouse?" asked the Captain. "Of *course* you'll ship with me. But first, I must have that package. Toddy, will you fetch it for me?"

"Aye, sir," I answered eagerly. I could already feel the deck of our new ship under my feet.

"That's the lad," said Captain Bones. "You'll find Captain Trapp sitting outside the Fogcutter Inn with the package in his hands. Now be on your way."

"You can count on me," I said. "I'll be back with the package within the hour." And I shot out of the warehouse like a cannonball.

The Underground Fort

It felt good to be in the warm sunshine after that damp, dark old warehouse. But I didn't dawdle along, just enjoying it. I had nearly a mile to cover, across town to the Inn, and I fairly flew down the cobblestone street.

Our own ship! I thought. At last I was really going to sea! It was about time too. I was nearly eleven.

Most of my friends had shipped out already, as cabin boys or deck hands on their fathers' whalers.

My uncle, Captain Bones, had sailed the sea on many a ship. Once, he had even been captain of his own whaling boat. That was many years ago, of course. It was hard to believe it, looking at him now. A damp, dark warehouse is no place for a seafaring man.

The years had been rough on my uncle. His clothes were ragged and dirty, and his beard was tangled like a bird's nest. As for me, I was growing up pale and skinny. And I was sick of the rats and the smell of moldy sacks in the warehouse. A ship was what both of us needed.

I reached Cod's Road and took a

shortcut across an empty lot. But I hadn't gone far when I heard someone shout my name.

"Tod!"

I wheeled about. It was my best friend, Billy Dobbs. All I could see was his head. It stuck out of a hole in the ground, like a gopher's.

"What are you doing?" I asked.

"Building a fort. Want to help?"

"I'm in a hurry," I said. "I have to pick up a package for my uncle."

"Then come back later," said Billy. "If you help, I'll let you live in the fort. It'd be nicer than that smelly warehouse."

"Thanks, but Captain Bones and I are about to get our own ship," I said. "We're going to be rich."

"Rich? Captain Bones?" laughed Billy. "Your uncle and his schemes! He's never had a penny and he never will. I'd like to see the day he gets rich."

"You'll see it sooner than you think. This time will be different!" I shouted, hurrying off.

Billy was almost as bad as the rest of the people in New Bedford when

it came to making fun of my uncle.
At least Billy called him Captain.
Most folks in town wouldn't even pay
him that much respect. They said

he'd never been more than a deck
hand. It pained me something awful
to hear them speak that way. I could
hardly wait to see their look of surprise, the day we sailed out of New
Bedford in our new ship. The thought
made me smile, and I ran the rest of
the way to the Inn.

At the Fogcutter Inn

An old sea captain, with a blue stocking cap on his head, dozed beside the door of the Fogcutter Inn. On the bench at his side was a small wrapped package, tied with heavy string.

"Excuse me," I said. "I've come for the package."

The captain opened an eye and squinted up at me.

"Now what package would that be?"

"I don't know, sir," I said. "My uncle just sent me to pick up a package from Captain Trapp at the Fog-cutter Inn. Are you Captain Trapp?"

Suddenly, the old sailor reached up and grabbed my arm. Before I could make a move, he had pulled me down to him.

"I'll ask the questions, lad," he said in a hoarse voice. "Now tell me, just who might your uncle be?"

"Captain Bones," I said shakily.

"And why didn't the Captain come himself?"

"It's his gout, sir," I said. "He can't move."

And neither can I, I thought, trying to break from the sailor's steely grasp.

The old sea captain snorted, but he let me go. "I suppose no one but Bones would send a boy halfway across New Bedford for the piece of junk in *this* package. I don't know what his game is. Does he think to sell it? If he's lucky, the most he'll get for it is a penny or two."

A penny or two! What kind of a

trick had my uncle played on me this time? What about our ship? He couldn't buy *that* with a penny or two!

Angrily, I grabbed the package. It felt kind of heavy, but not heavy enough to be money. As I hurried back to the warehouse, I thought that Captain Bones had a lot to explain, and I meant to get the truth from him, or else.

The Kidnapper

My trip back to the warehouse took even less time than my trip to the Inn. But when I got there, I stopped and stared. A strange black carriage was standing beside the door. I sneaked softly up to the wooden building and listened. Angry voices came from inside.

"Where's the Great Red Eye?" demanded a strange voice.

The Great Red Eye! Now that was a name I had heard before, though I couldn't remember where or when or even *who* had said it.

"I told you, it's not here, you yellow-bellied bilge rat." (That was the voice of my uncle, Captain Bones.)

"If you don't believe me, why don't you search the place?"

I peered through a grimy window. A tall, hatchet-faced man with a scar on his cheek was holding my uncle tightly by the shoulder.

"It would take me days to search this junk pile," said the stranger, looking around the cluttered warehouse.

"And there's no time for that. You're coming with me, Cap'n. Your tongue will loosen after you've been locked up a few days. No one will find you where *we're* going."

The hatchet-faced man must have been very strong, for he practically lifted Captain Bones off the floor.

I had to think fast. I couldn't let my uncle be kidnapped. A broken board was lying beside the warehouse, and I picked it up.

"I'll bean him the second he steps outside," I whispered, crouching behind the warehouse door.

The struggling men were moving toward the door. I tightened my sweaty hands around the board, and lifted it above my head. Then, sud-

denly, the door shot open. It caught me broadside and slapped me flat against the wall, almost knocking me out. Though dazed, I could hear my uncle's bellow of pain.

"Blast you, man! You've stepped on my gouty toe!"

Captain Bones was making such a racket it's a wonder the constable didn't hear him down in the town.

But by the time I managed to scramble from behind the door, Captain Bones had been dragged out and heaved into the carriage.

"If you value your life, you'll release me this instant," I heard him shout. "I'm not a man to be trifled with!"

Captain Bones was answered by the crack of the driver's whip.

The carriage lurched and clattered away.

I stood in the empty street with my mouth open. My head and my heart were pounding. I *wished* I could remember what I'd heard about the Great Red Eye.

What Was
in the Package

The man who kidnapped Captain Bones had looked dangerous as well as strong. If I was to free my uncle, I would need help. So, with the package securely under my arm, I set out for Billy Dobbs' fort.

"Why would anyone want to kidnap your uncle?" asked Billy when I told him what had happened.

We were sitting on the earth floor of Billy's fort. He'd dug a good wide hole, and the two of us fitted in nicely, with some room to spare.

"I think it has something to do with this package," I answered. "The Captain said it was going to make us rich."

"So that's where your ship money was coming from!" said Billy. "What is it, anyway?"

"I don't know," I confessed.

"Then let's open it," said Billy, reaching for the package. "It may give us a clue to the kidnapper."

I held onto the package. "Oh, I couldn't open this. It belongs to the Captain."

"Tod, that package is all we've got. We *have* to open it!"

Billy was right. If we were to find Captain Bones and free him, the package was where we would have to start. It was our only clue.

"All right," I said slowly. "But the Captain isn't going to like this."

Billy leaned forward.

I pulled off the string.

Then I took off the paper.

And then I pulled out what was inside.

It was a black cat made of solid plaster!

"A plaster cat?" asked Billy, unbelieving.

"A plaster cat?" I echoed. "Captain Bones must have slipped his anchor! This can't be worth anything — well, maybe a penny or two," I added, remembering Trapp's words. "It's probably a doorstop. It's heavy enough."

"I've seen dozens just like it," said Billy.

"So have I," I said. "It's no clue at all."

We sat in silence.

"No wonder everyone's always laughing at my uncle," I said, turning the cat over in my hands. "Sometimes he seems to have no more sense than — than a loony seagull."

I was about to toss the cat out of the fort, when something about it made me pause.

"Billy," I said. "Where have you seen cats like this before?"

"Eli Spoonbill's front yard is one place," said Billy. "He must have almost a hundred black plaster cats sitting there."

"Right. Now tell me, where else in New Bedford have you seen this cat?"

Billy cupped his chin in his hand and thought for a long time.

"I can't think of any other place," he said finally.

"Exactly," I said. "So you see there *is* something special about this cat, after all. It's the only one in New Bedford that's not in Eli's front yard."

"Do you think someone stole it from Mr. Spoonbill?" Billy asked.

"I don't know, but there's only one way to find out," I said. "And that's to go have a talk with Mr. Eli Spoonbill."

I boosted myself out of the fort. "Come on, Billy. Let's go."

The Mysterious
Mr. Spoonbill

Eli Spoonbill's house was a regular tourist attraction in New Bedford. For years Eli had been collecting plaster statues of cats. Each and every statue was the same — a black cat sitting up tall, with big green eyes. Eli had a pile of them. They filled his yard, they covered his porch, and they even sat on his roof. No one knew why he collected the cats. Most people thought he was crazy.

Though it was a bright sunshiny day, Eli Spoonbill's house looked dark and gloomy to us as we approached it.

"Are you sure you want to go in there?" asked Billy, as we started up the walk.

I stared at the silent black cats on either side of us. The cats stared back.

"We won't stay long," I promised. I knew Billy was scared. I was pretty scared, myself. "We'll leave as soon as we find out what Eli knows about this cat."

Just then, the big door to the house

began to open. I looked up, and in that
instant I tripped over a rough place in
the walk and nearly fell. The cat I was

carrying tumbled onto the lawn. It knocked the statues together in a pile of identical, black plaster pussycats.

"What's going on here?" a voice asked sharply.

I looked up. It was Eli Spoonbill. He looked just about as dark and gloomy as his house. Hurriedly, I picked up the cat and stood up.

"What are you trying to do?" he continued. "Steal one of my cats?"

"No, sir," I replied. "This cat belongs to me."

"Belongs to you?" he asked, raising a bushy eyebrow.

"Well not exactly to me, sir," I said. "It really belongs to my uncle, Captain Bones."

At the mention of Captain Bones,

Mr. Spoonbill suddenly broke into a wide grin.

"Why Captain Bones is one of my best friends. Tell me, how is he these days?"

"He's been kidnapped," I said. "I'm hoping you can help us find him."

Mr. Spoonbill looked really shocked at our news. "Kidnapped, you say? Why that's dreadful! Who could have done such a thing?"

He shook his head and said softly, "Of course I'll do everything I can to help you find your uncle, my boy. Now come inside. I want to hear all about it."

I followed Mr. Spoonbill, and Billy followed me, into the house. Eli led us into a big, high-ceilinged room, crowded with more black plaster cats. In one corner, I noticed a man bending over a broken cat. His back was toward us so we couldn't see his face.

"How would you boys like something to drink?" Eli asked. "Lemonade, perhaps?"

"Yes, sir," said Billy.

"I'll have some too," I said, liking Mr. Eli Spoonbill better and better.

"James!" called Mr. Spoonbill. "These boys here would like some lemonade."

The man in the corner turned around — my heart nearly stopped. James was the strange man who had kidnapped my uncle from the warehouse!

"Wait for me in the kitchen, James,"

said Mr. Spoonbill. "I'll help you squeeze the lemons."

"That's all right," said the man. "I can make the drink myself."

"I said, '*Wait for me in the kitchen,*'" repeated Mr. Spoonbill in a louder voice.

Then he turned to us and smiled reassuringly.

"Make yourselves at home," he said. "I'll be back in a minute."

The House
of the Black Cats

As soon as he was out of the room,
I started talking to Billy very fast.

"That's the man who kidnapped
my uncle. And Eli must be the one
who sent him! I'll just bet those two
didn't go into the kitchen to mix up
any lemonade. They're going to mix

up some trouble for us — like knock-out drops, or a plan to tie us up. I think Captain Bones — "

But Billy wouldn't let me finish. "Come on!" he urged. "Let's get out of here while we can!"

"We're not leaving without Captain Bones," I said firmly. "I think he's tied up somewhere in this house. Now's our chance to rescue him."

"There's no time," said Billy, nervously watching the kitchen door. "Spoonbill will be back any minute."

"Oh, come on!" I said. "Help me find Captain Bones. Please."

Billy didn't want to stay in that house a minute longer, but he *was* my friend. So the two of us started searching the house, throwing open

doors and poking into all kinds of funny, dark little closets. And every room we checked contained some of those black plaster cats. Eli must have had a hundred of them.

Once I thought I had found Captain Bones. But when I got closer, I discovered it was nothing but a pile of rags.

Captain Bones didn't seem to be anywhere in the house, and we were getting frantic. Any minute we expected those two to come back and catch us.

Finally, though, we opened the door of a tiny room at the back of the house and there he was, gagged and tied to a chair and looking mad as anything.

The Great Red Eye

"It's mighty good to see you, Toddy!" said my uncle as I freed him from the gag and ropes. "By the barnacles, I don't think those scoundrels would ever have set me free."

"Let's go!" I snapped. (I was still mad at him for getting us into this crazy cat caper.) "There's no time to lose.

Billy, Uncle Bones can't move very fast. Will you go ahead and see if the way is clear?"

Billy nodded. Moving cautiously, he left the room. But he hadn't taken three steps when he ran smack into Hatchet-face. James had been sneaking around too, trying to surprise us. He did.

"Now where would you be going?" he asked, clamping a heavy hand on Billy's shoulder. "You haven't had your lemonade yet."

"I . . . I decided I wasn't thirsty," stammered Billy. "Really, I must be going."

James tightened his grip on Billy and marched him back into the main room where Mr. Spoonbill stood grinning. Only this time his grin wasn't friendly.

"Now isn't this a cozy group!" he said. "I'm real glad you all stopped by to watch me break open the cat."

He turned to me. "You do still have the cat, don't you?"

The cat was on the floor. I bent down and picked it up.

"I've got it," I said. "But you can't have it. This cat belongs to my uncle, and I don't plan to give it up."

"That's the lad," said the Captain, glaring across the room at Spoonbill. "Don't let that bilge rat bully you."

I tightened my grip on the cat. Spoonbill reached for it.

"What's so special about this cat anyway?" I asked, putting it behind me. "There must be a hundred cats here. What do you care if my uncle has just one?"

"Because it's the only cat that holds the Great Red Eye, the biggest ruby in the world," said Captain Bones calmly. "Worth a sultan's ransom, that stone. Eli and I have been chasing after it for twenty years. I finally ran it down in New Orleans and had Captain Trapp bring it to me."

"A ruby!" I exclaimed. "How could

a ruby get into that cat? It's solid plaster!"

"Never mind. You've heard too much already," snapped Spoonbill. "Now give me that cat before I take it from you."

"You can't have it!" I said. "You've stolen your last cat."

Spoonbill's face turned red with anger. "The cats in this house are *not* stolen!" he shouted. "I bought them all. I had to."

"Why? Tell me why," I demanded.

Spoonbill sighed. "All right," he said. "You shall have your story. What do I care, now that the Great Red Eye is mine?"

Fixing his eyes greedily on the cat I held, he began:

"Years ago, Bones and I were sailors on the same ship, *The Golden Pike*. One of our shipmates, Billy Blades, stole the Great Red Eye from a museum in New York City. The guards chased Billy in and out of a dozen shops before they finally caught him. But when they did, the ruby was gone."

Captain Bones picked up the story at this point. "We learned later that Billy had run through a shop where plaster cats were made. Some of the statues weren't quite dry. So Billy pressed the ruby into the base of one. By the time Billy's story got out, the cats had been shipped all over the country. It's taken twenty years to find the right one."

"And how do you know this is the right one?" I asked.

"Because Billy Blades' cat has a dent in the bottom. It's Billy's thumbprint, to be exact," said Spoonbill.

I slipped my hand under the cat I held and felt along the base. I fully expected to come across Billy Blades' thumbprint. But I didn't. The bottom was perfectly smooth!

"Now, kindly hand over that cat," said Spoonbill. "Otherwise, I'll have to ask James to take it from you. And James is no gentleman when he takes things from people."

"If you want it, it's yours," I said. Then, before anyone could move, I whirled and threw it into a pile of Eli's cats.

"That's the boy!" snorted Captain Bones. "Make him work for his ruby."

The Chase

Eli Spoonbill was working as hard and as fast as he could. He dug into that pile of broken cats like a dog digging up a bone.

"Now's our chance to escape," I said in a low voice. "Captain . . . Billy . . . let's go!"

Billy was already out of the door, but Captain Bones didn't budge.

"Come on!" I shouted. But Captain Bones didn't even hear me. He was too busy laughing at his old shipmate, Eli Spoonbill.

I caught up with Billy at the front door. "Wait," I said. "We have to get the ruby."

"What do you mean?" asked Billy. "Isn't it back there in the pile of broken cats?"

"The cat I threw had a smooth base. I must have picked it up by mistake, thinking it was Uncle Bones', when I tripped earlier, coming up the walk. The one we want must still be on the lawn where I dropped it."

So while Spoonbill and James were madly pawing the cats inside, Billy and I were frantically searching

through the cats outside. Cats were flying everywhere. People on the street must have thought the Spoonbill cats had gone to war.

At last I found the right one. "Here it is!" I shouted, holding the precious cat over my head. "It's the one cat with Billy Blades' thumbprint!"

Eli Spoonbill must have heard my

shout. "Give it to me!" he yelled, bursting onto the porch.

"Run, Toddy!" shouted Captain Bones, coming up behind Spoonbill. "Don't let him get that ruby."

Billy and I took off. And Spoonbill and James came tumbling after us.

"To the fort!" I yelled, turning the corner and heading up Cod's Road.

We were racing at top speed but Spoonbill and James were gaining on us. I could hear the thud of their heavy feet coming closer, but I was going too fast to turn around.

We sprinted into the empty lot and raced for Billy's fort.

"Jump!" I yelled.

Side by side we leaped — but we leaped so far we sailed right over the hole and landed on the other side.

They've got us now, I thought. Good-bye ruby, good-bye ship.

But when we turned around, we were just in time to see James go crashing into that deep, wide hole. Mr. Spoonbill fell in on top of him, and the fall knocked them both senseless. (Without intending to, Billy had built a perfect booby trap!)

Billy and I shook hands. "Good work," I said to Billy.

"Good work," said Billy to me.

Stolen Goods

It wasn't long before Captain Bones came limping into the lot. A policeman was with him. The Captain peered into the hole and chuckled.

"There're your kidnappers," he said. "All ready for the brig."

The policeman lowered himself into the hole, although it was a tight fit.

"As soon as they come round, I'll take them in," he said. "You boys did a fine job." Then he handcuffed the unconscious prisoners.

I felt so good about capturing the kidnappers that for a moment I forgot all about the Great Red Eye. But not Captain Bones.

"Toddy, be a good boy and hand me that cat," he said. "Let's see what Billy Blades put away for us."

Captain Bones picked up the cat and knocked it against a rock. The plaster cat broke into a hundred pieces.

"Aha!" said Captain Bones, picking up a small object from the pile.

When Captain Bones held out his hand to us, we gasped and blinked.

Sparkling in the sunlight was the Great Red Eye itself, as bright as blood and as big as a robin's egg.

"Isn't she a beauty, though!" said Captain Bones, turning it round in the sun. "It's the prettiest stone I've ever seen."

"And the most valuable," I added. "It's beautiful, and the whaling ship she'll buy us will be even more beautiful. Right, Captain Bones?"

"Wrong!" said the policeman. He took the ruby from Captain Bones' hand. "Unless I'm mistaken, this is the Great Red Eye. It's stolen goods."

My heart sank. It was much worse to have had the precious ruby and then lost it, than never to have had it at all.

"However," the policeman added,

"I do believe there's a reward for the ruby's return."

My hopes rose.

"Quite a large reward."

My heart soared.

"With that reward money, we can build ourselves a fine little fishing boat," said Captain Bones. "What do we need a big whaler for anyway?"

"Will I still have a place on board?" I asked.

"By the barnacles, lad, didn't I tell you?" said the Captain. "You're going to be first mate!"

I looked up at Captain Bones and smiled. It had been a long time since I had felt this happy. Captain Bones looked down at me. And, though I couldn't really see his face behind all that beard, I knew he was smiling too.

THE END